D1389123

A killer bug has been set loose on Earth, with disastrous consequences. Professor Gamma and his daughter Kiryl, along with their young friend William, go to the Planet of Death to find the cure.

Geoffrey Hoyle

Fred Hoyle

Martin Aitchison

For Bo

Titles in Series 823
The Energy Pirate
The Frozen Planet of Azuron
The Giants of Universal Park
The Planet of Death

First edition

© LADYBIRD BOOKS LTD MCMLXXXII

THE PLANET OF DEATH

by Fred and Geoffrey Hoyle
illustrated by Martin Aitchison

Ladybird Books Loughborough

The Planet of Death

"They're beginning to die of it in China," William heard his father say from behind his newspaper, as they sat at the breakfast table. William glanced towards his mother, whose face clouded with worry as his father spoke.

Thoughtfully, William heaped another pile of cereal and milk onto his spoon and pushed the load firmly into his mouth. The past three weeks, he reflected, had not been enjoyable. He'd had too much time on his hands. School had been closed because of an epidemic, and William had had to keep quiet because his sister was ill too. Nobody seemed to know much about this new disease, which was called the French Ague – not even the specialists in London.

As William crunched through the last morsel of cereal, the front door bell rang suddenly, making him jump. His father and mother vanished from the room to answer the door, then he heard voices in the hall. Curious, he went quickly to the kitchen doorway. The doctor was speaking very seriously about William's sister. Her condition was getting worse, he feared. As William listened, he decided it was time for action.

At the back door, he stopped to pull on his wellingtons and an old anorak, then he set off for Wit's End, the ramshackle house of Professor Gamma and his daughter Kiryl. It lay deep in the wooded valley below the crest of the distant Down.

The house could not be seen from the Down, nor to William's knowledge from anywhere else. The locals even denied the existence of Wit's End, which William could never understand, because *he* knew exactly where to find it. He had to admit the house was well camouflaged, however, with ivy growing all over it, even over the doors. Not only that, the trees in the garden appeared to have been planted so that their tops and upper branches spread out over the roof, to hide the house from the air.

"Well, well, well!" boomed the Professor heartily, as he opened the back door.

"I'm sorry to bother you," William blurted out, "but my sister is very ill. She's got the French Ague, and I think she is going to die, like the Chinese."

"That is indeed grave news," Gamma rumbled, his face turning a bright pink. He held the door wide, and William followed him into the kitchen. It was much bigger than the kitchen at home, with a great black range at one end, flanked by two huge chairs. Into one of these the Professor dumped himself with a thud. William climbed up onto the seat of the other. It was surprisingly soft, and he sank back into it without even a rustle. Immediately all the normal outside sounds vanished, to be replaced by a total silence.

Professor Gamma stared at William for a moment or two, then he stuck his large-bowled pipe into his mouth and began to suck hard on the stem. William knew this to be a good sign, for it showed the Professor to be deep in thought on some problem. William hoped he was thinking about the strange new disease.

To occupy his time as he waited, William studied the man who sat opposite him. He was never quite sure what to make of Professor Gamma, for his appearance was never the same twice. He often had grey hair, but today it was brilliantly red and his pink face made him look younger. Gone were the wrinkles and stooped back which made him look old.

At last he spoke. "Sounds like Viro's work," he grunted.

"Viro?" puzzled William. "Who's Viro?"

"It!" corrected Gamma. "Went to school with It. Never liked It."

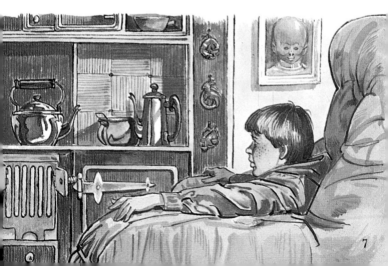

"Oh," said William thoughtfully, wondering if the Professor's use of the word 'it' could be the same as his own.

"If I remember rightly," boomed Gamma, "Viro became the curator of a terrible place called the Planet of Death."

William was startled by this strange piece of information. "I thought curators looked after museums?" he said.

"I suppose they do," replied Gamma, biting hard on the stem of his pipe. "Viro *is* a curator of a museum — a museum of disease."

"You mean this Viro," said William, (remembering it was an It), "has sent this ague thing to make us all ill?"

Professor Gamma nodded emphatically, causing his spine to snap loudly with each movement of his head.

William suddenly felt angry. "How do we stop him — er — It?" he asked.

"Too late to do that, I'm afraid," rumbled the pink-faced Professor. "But we *can* do the next best thing."

"What's that?"

"We will have to find the antidote to this so-called French Ague. Viro would never release a disease without knowing the cure. Otherwise it might die like the rest of us," growled Gamma with a grim laugh.

William nodded. It all sounded logical. At this moment he felt a great rush of air swirl about him. He

eased forward in the great chair to see what was happening. He saw Professor Gamma's daughter, Kiryl, shutting the back door of the house and walking towards them across the kitchen floor. As she came nearer he could see her mouth moving, but no sound seemed to come out of it. Then she sat down beside him on the chair, and he could hear her.

"Hello, William," she puffed as though she had run a long way. "I was sorry to hear about your sister," which made William wonder how she knew.

"How bad is it?" Professor Gamma asked his daughter.

"The disease is spreading rapidly, and it's serious. Young people seem to be affected first, followed by adults," Kiryl replied.

William was horrified by this statement. Not only was he about to lose his sister, he was going to lose his parents as well!

"Has anyone found a cure?" asked the Professor, scratching the end of his nose.

"No," replied Kiryl. "Staff from the medical research laboratories are all going down with the disease. It won't be long before everyone has it."

She looked gravely at William and the Professor followed her gaze. "It seems that our only remedy is to get the antidote," grunted the Professor.

"I don't fancy going to see Viro," Kiryl said in disgust.

"I think it's our only course of action," said her father, "because we don't seem to have much time."

There was no formal invitation to William: there never was. He always had the feeling that any decision was being left to him. He said, "Er . . ." but this seemed to satisfy Gamma, who stuffed his pipe into a pocket and got up from his huge chair.

They left the house by a front door: this was a routine which William had observed whenever they were embarking on a journey. It always puzzled him, for he'd never been able to find that particular door under the ivy.

It took him all his time to keep up with Gamma and Kiryl, but at length the three of them reached the top of the Down. The Professor took the giant pipe from his pocket and tapped it hard against his shoe before inserting it into his mouth.

William watched, as he always did, to see if he could discover how the trick was done. The Professor directed the bowl of his pipe skywards, and a deep scowl appeared upon his face. This was all part of communicating with a robot space-relay station far out on the other side of the Sun. The pipe, William knew, was really some kind of an energy-pipe. Microseconds later the air about them became alive, making William's ears pop madly.

If anyone had been watching they would have first seen three figures standing on an open hill top. Then in a space of time shorter than the blink of an eyelid the figures would have vanished. If the observer had really sharp eyesight, he would have seen a flash of coloured light, followed several moments later by a sound like the tearing of cloth. And if he had been curious enough to walk to the spot from which the three figures had vanished, he would have been surprised to find a hole some three metres across and one metre deep. He would have discovered that the ground at the bottom of the pit would still be too hot to touch.

The robot relay station supplied a great bolt of energy, and this produced instantaneous acceleration for the three passengers.

There was no point at which William felt the bolt rejoin the vast network of energy routes which run all over the universe. The only sign that he was being transported across space was the way all the stars appeared to be crowded together. Yet he knew they were really many light years apart from each other. Gamma had told him this phenomenon was due to the speed at which they travelled. Gamma had also told him that the energy routes were fuelled by black holes, which William didn't really understand.

Being dematerialised by the bolt of energy was a strange experience. Anybody outside an energy route could see nothing, but when you were travelling along inside the energy paths you could look out and see anybody trying to look in. To William it seemed the ideal way to be invisible!

He knew that somewhere within arm's length were the Professor and Kiryl. A cascade of red lights not far away indicated a deviation in the roadway.

"You'd think they'd have this thing straightened out by now," grumbled the Professor — he sounded just like William's father when he drove along the main road!

"It's going to be a rough one," called Kiryl in warning, as she dipped out of sight.

William watched in trepidation as he approached a monstrous cascade ahead. It was just as if they were going from the smooth surface of a high mountain lake into a river that descended to the valley below in a series of wild rapids. Light, predominantly red with flashes of blue, pulsated about them. Then suddenly they were thrown up and out, over a great waterfall which sparkled bright yellow.

They tumbled and turned in never-ending motion. The fall seemed to go on for ever, until at last they dropped into a swirling mass of white foaming light. William allowed his body to flow with the energy field as it curved and twisted through the warps of space.

Suddenly the great wall of white light burst into a spectrum of colours.

The instant they hit this new bump, they were hurled against the extreme edge of the energy field of the roadway. For a brief second William thought he was about to be thrown deep into space. Luckily the energy field was strong enough to suck them back again into the centre of the stream.

The tangled mass of alternating white and coloured light became worse, as the energy waves became completely confused. A dangerous place to be, thought William as he felt himself pulled in a million different directions. He knew that it was at times like this that it would be all too easy to lose a part of his body, getting it ripped off by the vast forces of confusion.

"Everyone all right?" asked Professor Gamma breathlessly.

"Think about where we are going . . ." started Kiryl.
Then — "Ohhhhhh."

Before any of them had time to speak again, they
began to elongate, as if they were being squeezed down
an ever-thinning tube.

Suddenly great sparks as big as footballs started
whizzing across their path. William felt his head must
be on one side of the galaxy while his feet were still at
the other side. Fortunately he was now so thin that the
giant sparks missed him.

The balls of dreadful energy stopped shooting across
his path just as abruptly as they had started. The route
now levelled off, with only a few remaining twists and
turns to overcome, and William relaxed. This was a
mistake, because suddenly he contracted just like an
elastic band snapping back to its normal length.

While this was happening he missed the arrival of a really giant warp which had been hidden below the horizon, and he saw it only at the very last moment. It was a little like a whirlpool jumping up at him from below, and as he went into it, his arms and legs flew in all directions.

The magnetic eddy currents of the warp were twisted like the strands of a rope, and they caused him to spin faster and faster as each moment went by. In the middle of this spinning problem he suddenly felt small pin pricks all over like a million tiny electric shocks.

"Are you all right?" Gamma suddenly asked, sounding far away.

"No," replied William feebly.

"Hang on!" shouted Kiryl. "I'm getting terrific feedback from the next robot station. I think it's deliberately trying to blast us apart."

"It must be Viro's work!" muttered the Professor. "Here, let me deal with that station."

Professor Gamma must have done something drastic, for the intense energy barrier set up by the robot station suddenly collapsed, and they found themselves coasting peacefully over a smooth plane. William felt very relieved — he'd had some very uncomfortable moments. Then — "Crash landing!" cried Gamma, and William braced himself once more.

"Viro's a clever villain," went on Gamma. "He had told that robot station we were a package of viruses on our way to infect the Universe."

"We are going much too fast," interrupted Kiryl. "We'll never materialise on impact."

"Stop fussing!" replied her father.

The robot station had plucked them from the main impulse road, firing them at great speed towards a dun-coloured planet that now came into view.

"Will it support life?" asked William, looking at the uninviting surface.

"Of course," replied the Professor cheerfully. "Same atmosphere as Earth — near enough, anyway. Watch out for the viruses and bacteria when we land."

"We are still going much too fast," warned Kiryl again.

Before another word could be uttered the three of them materialised — some one hundred metres above the planet's surface.

"*Now* see what you've done!" Kiryl shouted at her father in panic.

William stared down at the drab surface of the planet, waiting for the final plunge to what seemed almost certain destruction. To his surprise, however, they floated gently downwards as if suspended from parachutes.

"Gravity!" chortled Gamma. "If you studied harder you'd know about the gravity here."

William wondered why gravity should make any difference.

"What *is* the gravitational pull?" asked Kiryl sharply. She was cross with her father for teasing her.

"About a hundredth that of Earth's," grinned Gamma, gently tilting himself sideways. "Instead of plunging to the planet's surface at an acceleration of about ten metres per second in every second, we are calmly floating down at little more than ten centimetres a second in every second. Very civilised!" said Gamma.

Suddenly they heard a heavy clattering sound, like a

lot of stones banging together.

"Look there, Professor!" said William, pointing upwards. "What is it?"

Above them was a red flashing elongated ball, with yellow revolving circles at the front.

"Scarlet Fever, if I'm not mistaken," said the Professor, turning himself about to get a better look.

"What?" asked William in surprise.

"Definitely Scarlet Fever," came the reply. "A Scarlet Fever bug."

"Why is it so big?" asked William again.

"When gravity is so low, it allows things to be much larger than you'd ever find back on Earth," replied Gamma.

"Is it dangerous?"

"Yes, extremely dangerous," came Gamma's reply as at last they touched down gently on the planet's surface. "One nip from those teeth and you'd be very ill indeed in a day or two."

"How does Viro send bugs to different planets?" asked William. "I'm sure there's nothing that big on Earth."

"They travel the same way as we have done," answered the Professor, "and their size will depend on where they are going. On Earth they are microscopic, blending in naturally with the landscape. So for the Earth, Viro will naturally have to shrink them down quite a lot."

Gamma started off across the surface as he finished speaking, and William and Kiryl followed. They were surprised to find how difficult it was to catch up with the great figure of the Professor. They bounced along in an almost uncontrollable kangaroo hopping motion because of the low gravity.

They had not gone far when what seemed to be solid
rock in front of them changed into a mass of pink and
yellow fluid.

"Quick!" yelled the Professor, grabbing the pair of
them and jumping in a long steep arc to safety.

"What was that?" asked Kiryl in disgust.

"Some form of stomach bug," said her father as they
hurried on.

"I don't like this place," remarked Kiryl.

William agreed with her. The Planet of Death was certainly not the place for him!

A swishing sound made him turn quickly, just in time to see a purple and red puff ball drifting towards them. As it hit the ground some metres away the outer shell of the bug disintegrated, releasing hundreds of little purple and red bugs. Once more they leapt to safety just in time.

"Are you sure you know where we're going?" Kiryl asked her father.

"Of course!" came the reply. "There should be a bunker somewhere hereabouts."

Two hundred metres further on they came to a bright metal dome on the planet's surface. William watched as Professor Gamma, using something which looked like a credit card, opened a hidden door in the metal dome.

"I'm very glad we're safe," remarked Kiryl as the door closed behind them.

"Safe?" asked her father. "What from? The bugs or Viro?"

"Stop frightening us!" said Kiryl angrily.

"Frightening," muttered the Professor below his breath. "You don't know the meaning of the word yet." He pulled himself to his full height (which seemed to be several centimetres taller than when they left Earth), and stalked off, Kiryl and William just behind him. As they came to the end of a short corridor, there in front of them was a blue illuminated hole.

"Remember not to talk to strangers," Gamma remarked, stepping out into the abyss before him. William and Kiryl watched in alarm as the Professor's head vanished completely from sight.

"He's quite crazy at times," said Kiryl — and she also stepped into the hole. William grabbed at her but he was too late. Instead, he overbalanced and plunged headlong into the empty space.

Once again he expected to fall heavily, but once again he floated like a feather downwards, in a steady tumbling motion which he could do nothing about. He did not notice Gamma and Kiryl standing on a ledge at one side, but the Professor grabbed his coat quickly and pulled him over beside them.

"How do we get up?" asked William, once he was firmly established on his feet.

"Things that come down," said the Professor with an airy wave of his pipe, "must also go up again. Otherwise everything that came down would be down here, not up there, if you get my meaning."

William didn't. He was about to say so when the wall behind them suddenly opened, and they walked through into a long passageway.

At length they emerged into a vast hall, and William moved forward tensely, wondering when they were going to meet Viro.

"Hurry," urged the Professor. "There's a circle marked on the floor. We have to find it."

William saw it first — a circle marked out on the

floor in a dull coloured metal. "There," he cried, pointing to the very centre of the hall.

"Good lad," puffed the Professor when they all arrived inside the circle. "Now remember, you mustn't step outside this metal boundary. Not in any circumstances whatever. If you do, they'll blow us into a cloud of dust."

As he spoke, forty or more huge giants came into the
hall. At first sight of the advancing monsters, William
moved closer to the Professor.

The creatures that moved soundlessly into a circle
around them were six metres tall. Their bodies
resembled tree trunks, being straight up and down and
a metre thick. On top of each tree trunk was a
spherical ball, with a disc of coloured light in the
centre. As the monsters came to a halt William noticed

that each one had a long tube at one side — and every
tube was pointing at the circle.

"Who are they?" whispered William. He wondered
how they moved about without legs.

"They are the guardians of the planet," replied the
Professor. "The guardians of disease."

"Why aren't they all dead?" asked William, bending
down to see if they ran on wheels.

"Idiot!" said Kiryl. "Can't you see they're robots?"

"Oh!"

"I wonder which is the foreman," mused the Professor, chewing at the stem of his energy-pipe.

"It must be that thing," said William, pointing. They all watched as a closed box with a spike sticking out from one of its faces floated through the air to a halt just short of the circle.

"It is a messenger," agreed Gamma. "We must identify ourselves."

He produced from his pocket the same card with which he had opened the metal dome at the planet's surface. He stepped forward and pushed the card firmly into a slit cut into the face of the floating box. There was a sucking noise and the card vanished. Suddenly the spike on the box waved backwards and forwards, and immediately a sliding door far across the hall began to open. They saw another hall beyond.

"Is this where we meet Viro?" asked William.

"For our sakes, I hope not!" said the Professor. "According to information I've gathered from the messenger, Viro is away on business."

"How did you know what to give the box?" asked William.

"My card is an all-purpose one," replied Professor Gamma. "It picked up exactly the identification they were looking for."

At a signal from the floating box with the waving

spike, the great robots formed two lines through which the three travellers had to walk to reach the next hall. As they moved forward, a swishing noise made William turn. He saw one of the robots aiming its tube at the doorway they were about to enter. When they reached the door, there on the ground lay a small green cube.

"Pneumonia," explained the Professor as they walked carefully over the dead bug.

In the next hall, they found another circle marked in the floor.

"What are these circles for?" asked Kiryl.

"It's a sort of no-man's land, where the robots may not attack us," replied her father.

William searched the room with his eyes, but there was no one there. Then, without warning, at the far end, a throne came up from the floor to rise to a height of about three metres above them. William was so curious he nearly stepped from the circle, but the Professor grabbed him. From the top of the throne a formidable creature that buzzed like a bluebottle rose into the air. It had a black pear-shaped body covered by a red flashing cap. It had no head, only two long stalks, one with a yellow ball on the end, the other with a red ball. These long antennae were constantly in motion, twisting and turning and gyrating.

William shivered as he took in the full horror. "What *is* that?" he gulped.

"Viro's director of laboratory operations," Gamma replied.

"I wish they just kept the antidotes here and not all these creatures and diseases," William muttered, staying close to the Professor.

"Don't be silly!" remarked Kiryl. "You can't make an antidote if you don't have the disease."

"Don't squabble," the Professor said crisply. "We have more than enough on our hands with this thing to contend with."

"I'm glad we came on a day when Viro was out!" said William.

The creature floated towards them, and stopped at the edge of the circle. The red cape that covered its back crackled continuously as it moved about them. The two antennae continued their strange dance.

William looked up at the Professor and saw that the energy-pipe was glowing cherry red with heat. The creature in front of them suddenly quivered frantically for an instant, then seemed to fall inside the circle. There was a big flash, a sharp crack and a horrible burning smell, then − nothing.

"Did you have to be as drastic as that?" asked Kiryl.

"No option," replied Gamma. "The thing had started to communicate with Viro."

Several doors were opening and closing now as if confusion reigned. Through one, William spied a laboratory with piles of instruments scattered about the room. When he pointed it out, the Professor nodded and said: "You two go ahead." As he spoke a great cloud of white gas belched forth from his pipe, laying down a very effective smoke-screen.

"He'll overdo it badly one of these days," Kiryl muttered as she and William moved quickly to the doorway of the laboratory.

"Will Viro come now that it has been told we are here?" asked William.

"Let's hope it doesn't arrive before we leave," Kiryl replied.

William was about to ask what Viro looked like, when the Professor joined them. "In we go," he said, leading the way.

Once inside the laboratory he shut the door and ran his pipe over the lock. "I've altered the opening combinations," he grinned. "That should keep those robots busy for a while!"

"Let's find the antidote and get out of here!" Kiryl said urgently.

Something nudged William's elbow, which made him freeze in fright. Then he looked down to see a black tray hovering at his side.

"That's very interesting!" cried the Professor, eyeing the tray.

"Phew!" said William in relief. "I thought it might be Viro."

The black tray nudged William again, tilting itself a number of times as if it was beckoning him.

"It wants you to follow it," explained Gamma.

The tray floated ahead of them down a corridor between great work benches. Some of the benches were covered in equipment, while others were quite empty.

Right in the centre of the room stood a vast platform on which there was an enormous chair. The Professor, puffing hard upon his pipe, climbed onto the platform and up into the chair. William stared in fascination, for the Professor could hardly climb onto the seat of the chair, it was so huge. If the normal occupant was Viro, what size must it be? Walking about on the chair the Professor was just able to reach to the top of the arm and to press large buttons on what was evidently a computer control unit.

Instantly the laboratory came to life. Liquids bubbled and gurgled in their retorts. Microscopes lit up, centrifuges whizzed, counters clicked loudly. The whole room was more like a magician's cave than a laboratory.

Professor Gamma hardly noticed what was going on below him, for he was programming the computer.

"What's taking so long?" shouted Kiryl impatiently after a few minutes.

"My dear," her father called down, "we are searching for the proverbial needle in a haystack.

We don't know what the disease is or where to find the antidote. All I can do is reduce the search systematically," he shouted again.

Moments later they were startled by a great voice booming out above the noise of the laboratory machinery. "Where are those humans?" it bellowed.

Then the heavy metal door began to bend.

"Maybe it's time we left," suggested William uneasily.

"Certainly not," the Professor shouted down at him. "We must get the antidote."

"Well, you'd better find it quickly," cried Kiryl sharply. "Very quickly indeed."

"Are we going to give up?" asked the Professor. He stared down at his two companions as the door began to give way.

William remembered his sister ill in bed at home, and defiantly cried "No!"

"That's better," approved Gamma. "We do have some advantage while I have control of the computer."

Then the voice barked, "Humans! I'll teach them not to meddle in my affairs." The metal door started to glow a bright red, then a harsh white. At last with a sharp crack it vanished completely.

Professor Gamma went on frantically tapping instructions to the laboratory computer through the console on the arm of the chair. A shower of sparks burst from the gap where the door had been. Every time one of the huge robots tried to come through the door it was melted into a bright puddle of metal by the sparks.

"While the power lasts," rumbled the Professor, "we are ahead of the game."

William craned his neck round the corner of a bench in an effort to see through the open doorway. But no matter how hard he tried, he caught no glimpse of Viro.

"I'll give Viro a little of its own medicine," roared the Professor, pushing still more instructions into the computer at lightning speed.

Instantly the black tray shot off across the room to return with a pile of red and white polka-dotted balls.

"What are they?" asked William.

"Virulent red-flu virus," answered Gamma. "In a matter of moments they will unfreeze and become highly active."

The tray moved quickly away to the distant doorway and through into the adjoining passage.

Suddenly a robot appeared in the doorway — and no sparks were there to destroy it.

"Power drain," the Professor gasped. "Viro is taking over, I'm afraid."

Before they had time to take cover, bolts of coloured light arched across the room. One narrowly missed the Professor, who dropped hastily off the seat of the chair.

"I didn't need much more time," he puffed, jumping down to join William and Kiryl on the floor.

More robots appeared, waving their electron guns. Bolts tore into the room, smashing equipment, ricocheting off tables and burning holes in the walls.

Kiryl turned to her father. "Let's go," she said decisively.

The tray was the first to move, vibrating itself to show them that they should follow. Half-crawling, half-running, they moved between the benches until they reached the furthest end of the laboratory.

"Stop running, humans! There is nowhere for you to go," boomed Viro's voice from very near at hand.

The tray stopped at a vast glass panel in the wall. The Professor waved his energy-pipe over the operating switch and the panel slowly started to lift itself open.

William turned to look back down the laboratory and then froze in horror at what he now saw. Coming through the doorway was a vast black jelly-like mass.

Sparks burst forth from its surface as it rubbed against the door pillars. At length the whole creature was through into the laboratory. It was a massive blob of vibrating slime. Suddenly it changed shape faster than the eye could follow. In one instant it was tall and thin, and then in the next it vanished as it spread itself quickly in a film across the floor.

"Wh...Wh...Wh...What is that?" asked William when he could get the words out.

Nobody spoke, for even as they watched a giant red ball began rolling over the surface of the black mass. Pinpoints of yellow light shone like eyes from the red ball and a terrifying crashing sound was emitted as if great teeth were crunching up rocks like a crushing plant in a quarry.

"That is Viro," the Professor said calmly, pulling them into the space behind the opening glass panel. Then he operated the closing mechanism with his pipe, and the panel began to close slowly. William could already feel air rushing upwards for some of it went up his trouser legs making his clothes flap. Looking up he saw a tunnel above their heads, and he wondered how they could climb up its vertical sides.

Through the glass panel they could see the great black mass, its fiery red head spinning wildly in search of them. The film of slime was oozing through the benches.

"You'll not get far," roared Viro furiously.

The updraught in the great fume cupboard where they were standing grew stronger and stronger now that its glass door was closing.

"The tray!" cried the Professor, so suddenly that he made William jump.

William looked through the glass door and saw the tray hovering outside. It was carrying a small blue sphere.

"It's the antidote!" yelled Kiryl. "The computer must have found it!"

Quickly William dropped to his knees, seizing the tray and pulling it into the cupboard through the ever-narrowing gap between the glass door and the floor. At the same moment a flying ball of red-flu bug fixed itself firmly to his arm.

"Ouch!" he cried in pain. Immediately the tray

turned lengthways and swatted the bug so hard it fell dead to the floor.

Just as the glass door clicked tightly shut, the huge black mass of Viro fell against it, blocking out all the light. The draught of air generated by Gamma's pipe was now so strong, however, that it sucked them up and blew them out on to the surface of the planet. In the next instant they were swept upwards by a bolt of energy to join the road for the journey home.

"I'm glad that's over," William said with a sigh.

"Not a place for a holiday?" grinned the Professor.

But then, just as they all thought themselves well clear of the Planet of Death, they caught sight of a black patch flying through space not far behind them. Suddenly great blue flashes came shooting past them, and once again they could hear the crashing boom of Viro's voice, "I'll roast you alive, humans! You'll not get far!"

Suddenly they felt as if they had been slammed into a solid wall. The effect was to glance them at an angle from the path they were following. There before them lay a great fiery star which burnt with a brilliance that was dazzling.

"Brace yourselves," whispered the Professor.

The relentless heat from the star was becoming unbearable. William could almost smell his flesh burning, when without warning they shot down a long funnel which drew them into a needle shape. Just when William had grown accustomed to this shape he found himself suddenly bent at ninety degrees in the middle, so that his body had become like a street corner.

A vast cascade of exploding sparks ended their ordeal.

"That should give Viro something to occupy itself with," Gamma remarked breathlessly.

"Aaaaaaaah!" William heard Viro cry. Looking behind, he saw a long thin black needle stretched out across the heavens. Suddenly the needle shot away out of sight. Then as William turned back to his companions, they hit a switchback of energy warps which never stayed in the same place for more than an instant at a time. It was just like driving up a shaking mountain road at breakneck speed. Fortunately, when they reached the top the disturbances ceased, leaving them a pleasant run home.

"What happened to Viro?" asked William at last.

"Viro's on its way across the Universe," laughed Gamma. "Luckily for us I happened to remember that fork in the route. Otherwise we would also be on an express loop to the far side of the Universe."

Going home seemed faster than William remembered the outward journey to have been. They landed as usual in a heap on the top of the Down outside his home village. The hole which they had left behind had become filled in, and the grass at that particular place had changed colour. It was blue now.

Rain was falling heavily. By the time they reached the shelter of the wood above the house they were all wet through. So preoccupied were they with the rain it wasn't until they had almost reached the house that Kiryl remembered the tray and the blue sphere. Running back, William found the tray bobbing along just above the ground. It was still carrying the blue sphere. The tray itself was damaged, with holes through its surface. William picked it up and ran after the others.

"Never be quite the same again," muttered the Professor, inspecting the tray carefully as they went into the house. "But a good sunny day will revive its spirits. Plenty of energy, that's what it will need." He handed it to William.

"Will the antidote still work?" asked William anxiously.

"Of course," nodded the Professor as he led the way into the kitchen. It was only then that William realised that he'd passed through the front door yet again without taking note of its exact position in the house wall.

The Professor held up the blue sphere with his left hand. Part of his middle finger was missing.

"I'm sure I had it this morning," he said, frowning.

They all examined themselves but he seemed to be the only person to have suffered from the journey.

"Part of a finger," he muttered. "I suppose it could have been worse. It's probably still being pursued across the Universe by Viro."

At this remark they all laughed.

"Never mind, father," smiled Kiryl, "we'll find you another piece of finger."

"Here I am complaining about a bit of a finger when there is important work to be done urgently. We must get this antidote to the Medical Research Council without delay," Gamma exclaimed.

William looked up at the grandfather clock in the corner. It read fifteen minutes past one o'clock. "I'll be late for lunch," he said, turning to go. Then as he hurried to the edge of the garden, he heard Kiryl calling after him.

"You forgot this," she said when she caught up with him. William took the pocket calculator she held out to him.

"What is it?" he asked, puzzled.

"It's the control unit for the tray," she smiled.

"Of course," he muttered, feeling he should have known something as simple as that.

"Your sister's going to be better soon," said Kiryl encouragingly as she turned away to run back to the house.

William stumped on home through the rain with the tray tucked beneath his arm.

"Look at you," scolded his mother as he went inside. "You're wet through — and just *what* is the matter with your hair?"

William touched his head. His hair was still there, but to his surprise it was very tightly matted.

"Upstairs with you and get those wet clothes off," his mother urged as he shook his wellingtons off by the back door.

He was thankful to escape so easily from his mother's questions. Like a flash he raced upstairs to the safety of his bedroom, where he placed the tray and its control unit carefully under his pillow. Then he turned to the mirror to inspect his hair. The colour was about right and so was the length. The problem was that the hair was matted together, and neither brush nor comb would part it. Thinking back, he decided that one of those bolts of energy fired by the robots must have fused the hairs together.

The doctor came the following morning to tell them that a marvellous cure for the French Ague had been found in London. William's parents were so relieved by this news that even his father forgot to keep on talking about the terrible state of his hair.

William went that afternoon to the village hairdresser, where he had all the offending hair removed. This left him with a savage crew-cut which annoyed his mother even more than his father!

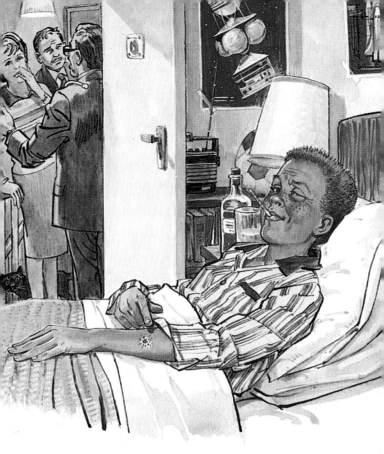

Three days later William came down with what the doctor thought at first to be the French Ague. But when swabs from William's throat were tested at the hospital laboratory the specialists found that William was suffering from red flu, not the French Ague. They were all astonished, because, as the doctor explained to William's mother, "Nobody has had the red flu for twenty years. We can't think where he got it from!"